The Babka Sisters

For Aunt Judy—with my best love and a billion babkas!
—L.N.

To all the siblings who cherish each other
—T.B. & T.B.

ACKNOWLEDGMENTS

A huge thank-you to baker extraordinaire Aaron Hamburger for creating Hester and Esther's delicious Best Babka in the World recipe, and to our babka testers, Everett Bradley, Peggy Gillespie, Lisa Herrick, Lori Stec, and Sky Vanderlinde for trying them out!

Recipe and photographs by Aaron Hamburger

KAR-BEN PUBLISHING®
An imprint of Lerner Publishing Group, Inc.
241 First Avenue North
Minneapolis, MN 55401 USA
Website address: www.karben.com

Main body text set in DIN Neuzeit Grotesk Std.
Typeface provided by Adobe Systems.

Library of Congress Cataloging-in-Publication Data

Newman, Lesléa, author. | Bobokhidze, Tika, illustrator. | Bobokhidze,Tata, illustrator.
Title: The babka sisters / Lesléa Newman ; illustrated by Tika and Tata Bobokhidze.
Description: Minneapolis, MN : Kar-Ben Publishing, [2023] | Includes recipe. | Audience: Ages 3–8. | Audience: Grades 2–3. | Summary: "Dueling baker sisters Esther and Hester meet their new neighbor Sylvester, who gladly becomes their babka tester, determining which shvester's (sister's) babka is the best"— Provided by publisher.
Identifiers: LCCN 2022015405 (print) | LCCN 2022015406 (ebook) | ISBN 9781728445564 (lib. bdg.) | ISBN 9781728445571 (pbk.) | ISBN 9781728481043 (eb pdf)
Subjects: CYAC: Jewish cooking—Fiction. | Sisters—Fiction. | Sibling rivalry—Fiction. | Sabbath—Fiction. | Jews—Fiction. | LCGFT: Picture books. | Fiction.
Classification: LCC PZ7.N47988 Bab 2023 (print) | LCC PZ7.N47988 (ebook) | DDC [E]—dc23

LC record available at https://lccn.loc.gov/2022015405
LC ebook record available at https://lccn.loc.gov/2022015406

Manufactured in China
1-1008816-51417-9/7/2022

0523/B2197/A5

The Babka Sisters

Lesléa Newman

illustrated by Tika and Tata Bobokhidze

KAR-BEN
PUBLISHING

Esther and Hester were sisters who lived next door to each other and adored each other.

"You're a doll," called Esther to Hester.
"You're a peach," called Hester to Esther.
And that's the way it was.

One summer evening, Esther rocked on her front porch with Lester purring in her lap and Hester swung on her front porch with Chester snoring at her feet.

"Hester, do you see what I see?" asked Esther, pointing to a window across the way.

"Yes," said Hester. "Someone has moved into the little blue house across the street."

"I'm going to bring them a babka for Shabbat," said Esther to Hester. "After all, *I* bake the best babka in the world."

"I'm going to bring them a babka for Shabbat," said Hester to Esther. "After all, *I* bake the best babka in the world."

And the great Babka Bake-Off was on!

Esther gathered and mixed.

Hester assembled and stirred.

Esther split and filled.

Hester divided and spread.

Esther and Hester baked.

Esther's house smelled like a celebration.

Hester's house smelled like a holiday.

"One bite of this babka will make our new neighbor dance with delight," said Esther to Lester as she pulled her babka out of the oven.

"One taste of this babka will make our new neighbor jump for joy," said Hester to Chester as she pulled her babka out of the oven.

Esther and Lester and Hester and Chester paraded across the street.

"Why don't you ring the bell? Can't you see my hands are full of the best baka in the world?" Esther scowled at Hester.

"Why don't *you* knock on the door? Can't you see my hands are full of the best babka in the world?" Hester scowled at Esther.

Chester growled at Lester.

Lester yowled at Chester.

The door opened.

"I am Esther, and *I* have brought you the best babka in the world."

"I am Hester, and *I* have brought you the best babka in the world."

"I am Sylvester, and I will be your babka tester."

Esther and Lester and Hester and Chester marched inside.

Esther cut.

Hester sliced.

Esther offered Sylvester
a gigantic serving.

Hester offered Sylvester
an enormous helping.

Sylvester tested Esther's babka and danced with delight. "Heavenly," he declared.

"Ha!" Esther beamed.

Sylvester tested Hester's babka and jumped for joy. "Out of this world," he declared.

"Ha!" Hester glowed.

But whose babka was the best?

"Esther!" cried Sylvester. "Your *shvester*, Hester, makes the best CHOCOLATE babka in the world."

"Hester!" cried Sylvester. "Your *shvester*, Esther, makes the best CINNAMON babka in the world."

Esther tasted Hester's babka and jumped for joy. "Marvelous," she proclaimed.

Hester sampled Esther's babka and danced with delight. "Magnificent," she pronounced.

Lester and Chester pestered Sylvester until he gave them each a big bite of babka.

And then it was time to light the candles for Shabbat.

Sylvester, Esther, and Hester sang the blessings over the candles, the challah, and the wine.

Chester howled proudly. Lester meowed loudly.

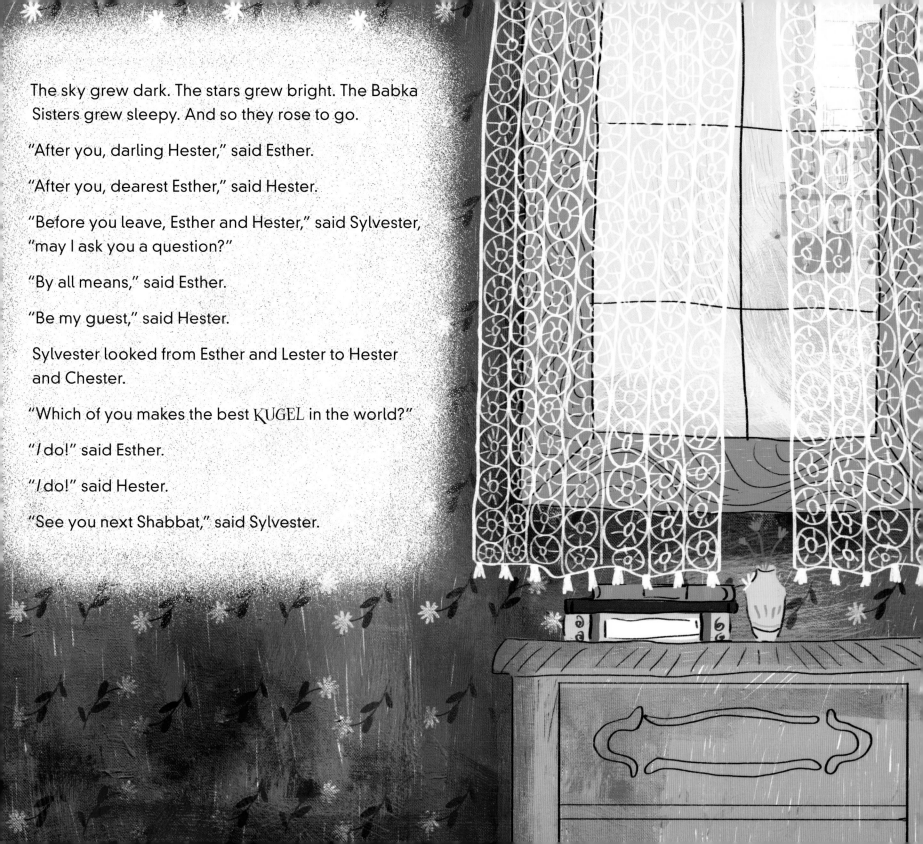

The sky grew dark. The stars grew bright. The Babka Sisters grew sleepy. And so they rose to go.

"After you, darling Hester," said Esther.

"After you, dearest Esther," said Hester.

"Before you leave, Esther and Hester," said Sylvester, "may I ask you a question?"

"By all means," said Esther.

"Be my guest," said Hester.

Sylvester looked from Esther and Lester to Hester and Chester.

"Which of you makes the best KUGEL in the world?"

"*I* do!" said Esther.

"*I* do!" said Hester.

"See you next Shabbat," said Sylvester.

And the great KUGEL cook-off was on!

The Best Babka in the World

Making babka is a fun project that needs a lot of resting time for your dough **overnight**, so plan ahead. (If you're feeling impatient, buy frozen challah dough to use instead of homemade!)

This recipe makes one loaf. You can make Hester's babka by choosing the chocolate filling, or bake Esther's babka by selecting the cinnamon filling. Either way, you'll bake the best babka in the world!

Make sure an adult is present to help you with using knives, a hot cooktop, and a hot oven.

EQUIPMENT

measuring cups

stirring spoons

stand mixer or electric mixer fitted with a dough hook OR a large bowl and wooden spoon

bowls for mixing fillings

plastic wrap

5 x 9 (13 x 23 cm) inch loaf pan

parchment paper

rolling pin

skinny spatula or butter knife

baking rack for cooling

INGREDIENTS

Dough

1/2 cup whole milk, room temperature

pinch plus 1/4 cup sugar

1 envelope (2¼ teaspoons) active dry yeast

2 cups plus 1/2 cup flour

1/2 teaspoon kosher salt (or 1/4 tablespoon table salt)

1 teaspoon lemon zest

1 egg plus 1 egg yolk

1/2 teaspoon vanilla

5 tablespoons unsalted butter, room temperature, cut into small cubes

Chocolate Filling

4 tablespoons unsalted butter

1/3 cup unsweetened cocoa powder

1/3 cup sugar

pinch of kosher salt

3 ounces semisweet chocolate, chopped fine

OR

Cinnamon Filling

4 tablespoons unsalted butter

1/2 cup brown sugar, packed

1 tablespoon flour

pinch of kosher salt

1 tablespoon cinnamon

Streusel Topping

2 tablespoons flour

1 tablespoon sugar

1 tablespoon brown sugar, packed

1/4 teaspoon cinnamon

pinch of kosher salt

2 tablespoons unsalted butter, room temperature, cut into cubes plus 2 tablespoons unsalted butter, melted

1/3 cup of mini chocolate chips (if making chocolate babka)

Simple Syrup

1/4 cup sugar

1/4 cup water

DIRECTIONS

1. Pour milk into a liquid measuring cup. Then sprinkle it with a pinch of sugar and the yeast. Stir lightly and let sit for 5 to 10 minutes, until tiny bubbles and a thin foam form on the milk surface.

2. In the bowl of a stand mixer fitted with a dough hook (or a large bowl if mixing by hand), mix 2 cups flour, salt, and lemon zest.

3. In a medium bowl, lightly beat eggs, sugar, and vanilla. Then add foamed yeast mixture and stir to combine. Add this wet mixture to the flour, and stir with the dough hook on low speed to combine, about 5 minutes. Once the mixture is moistened, raise the speed to medium and add the butter, one cube at a time. (If mixing by hand, mix the ingredients in a large bowl with a wooden spoon.)

4. Continue mixing until the dough is completely mixed and smooth. If too sticky, add some of the 1/2 cup of flour, a couple of tablespoons at a time. The dough should be somewhat tacky but should just come off the sides of the bowl. (If mixing by hand, turn out the moistened dough on a floured counter and gradually knead in the butter, dusting lightly with reserved flour if sticky.)

5. Place the finished dough in a lightly greased bowl covered with plastic wrap, and put it in the refrigerator overnight so the yeast can develop its flavor.

6.  The next day, remove the dough from the refrigerator (it may not look much bigger—that's okay) and let it sit on the counter for half an hour so it's soft enough to roll out but not too soft, or it'll stick as you roll it out.

7. In the meantime, make your filling of choice.

8. For chocolate filling: Melt butter, cocoa powder, sugar, salt, and bittersweet chocolate together, either in a small saucepan over low heat on the stove or in a microwave-proof bowl in the microwave, heating at 30-second intervals until combined into a spreadable paste. Be careful not to overheat the chocolate!

9. For cinnamon filling: Melt the butter. Mix in a small bowl with brown sugar, flour, salt, and cinnamon until combined into a spreadable paste.

10. Grease the loaf pan, and line it with a long sheet of parchment, enough for an overhang on both sides. (You'll use this as a sling to remove the baked babka later.)

11.  On a lightly floured surface, roll out the babka dough to a 12 x 16-inch (30 x 41 cm) rectangle, about 1/4–1/8-inch (6/10 to 3/10 cm) thick. If the dough is still cold from the refrigerator, beat it with your rolling pin to soften it. With an offset spatula or butter knife, spread the filling on the dough in an even layer, leaving a 1/2-inch (about 1 1/4 cm) border on all sides. You may have a bit of extra filling left over, depending on how thinly you rolled your dough.

12.  Starting from the longer side, carefully roll up the dough, moving slowly and tightly so you get as many layers as possible.

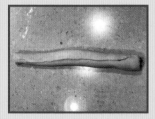

13.   When the dough is fully rolled up, use a long, sharp knife to cut down the middle lengthwise, so the filled layers are showing. Lay one long piece of dough crosswise on top of the other to form the letter X. Then braid the two strands.

14. Carefully place the coiled babka inside the loaf pan, and cover it with a clean, damp dish towel. Let the babka rest on the counter, about 1½ hours, so it can rise slightly.

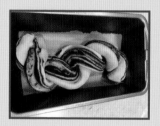

15. Meanwhile, make simple syrup. Stir together 1/4 cup sugar and 1/4 cup water in a small saucepan, and warm it over medium heat on the stove, stirring occasionally, until sugar is completely dissolved. Set aside to let cool.

16. Preheat oven to 350°F (177°C), and make streusel topping, combining first six ingredients with a fork into a rough crumble. Melt 2 tablespoons butter, and use it to brush the top of your babka. Crumble bits of the topping onto the babka. If making a chocolate babka, also top with chocolate chips.

17. Bake the loaf for 40 to 45 minutes until firm and browned on top.

18. Remove baked babka from the oven, and leaving it in the pan, set it on a rack and brush all over with the simple syrup. Let it cool until warm, 10 to 15 minutes.

19. Grab the edges of the parchment sling to remove the babka to cool completely on a baking rack.

20. Slice and enjoy! A well-wrapped babka is good for two days on the counter. You can also freeze it, well wrapped, for up to six months.

GLOSSARY

babka: a dense, loaf-shaped coffee cake sweetened with cinnamon or chocolate (either of which is absolutely delicious)

kugel: a sweet or savory baked pudding made with noodles or potatoes

shvester: the Yiddish word for "sister"

ABOUT THE AUTHOR

LESLÉA NEWMAN has created 80 books for readers of all ages. Her awards include two National Jewish Book Awards, the Massachusetts Book Award, and the Sydney Taylor Body-of-Work Award. She lives in Holyoke, Massachusetts.

ABOUT THE ILLUSTRATORS

TIKA AND TATA are sisters like the Babka Sisters! They live in the country of Georgia, and both have a passion for drawing. Their illustrations include many different techniques, using various colors and styles. Their work combines digital medium and hand-drawn textures.